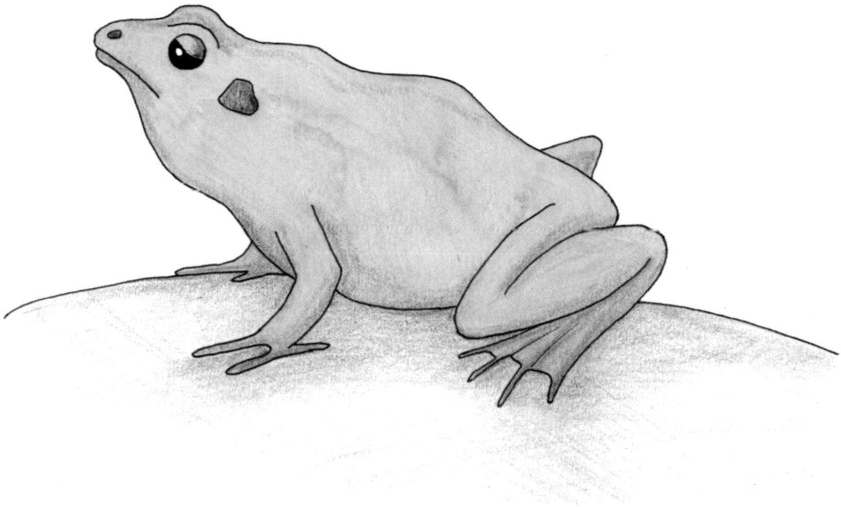

I am a frog.

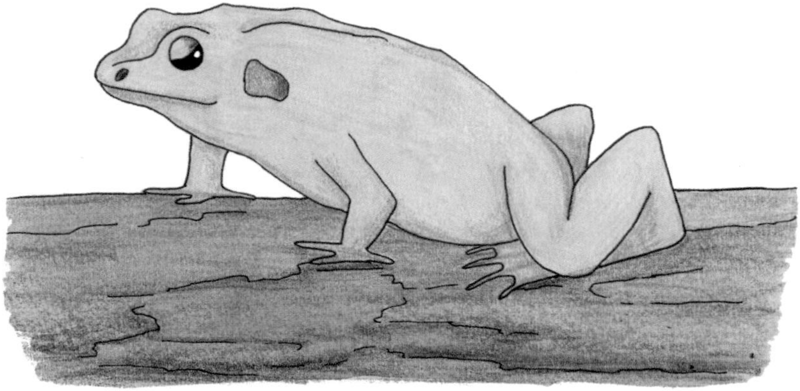

I am on a log.

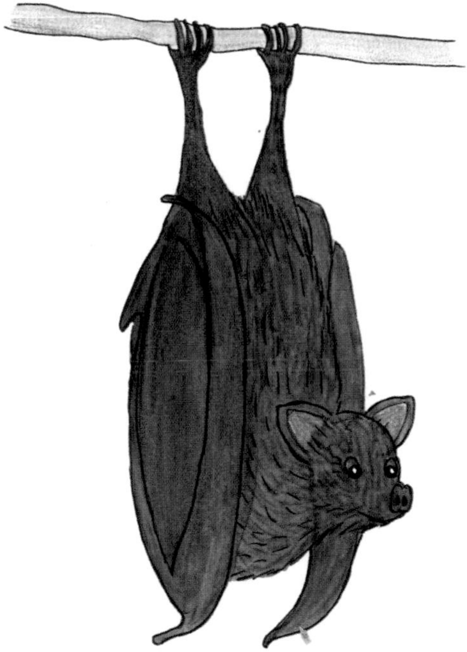

I am a bat.

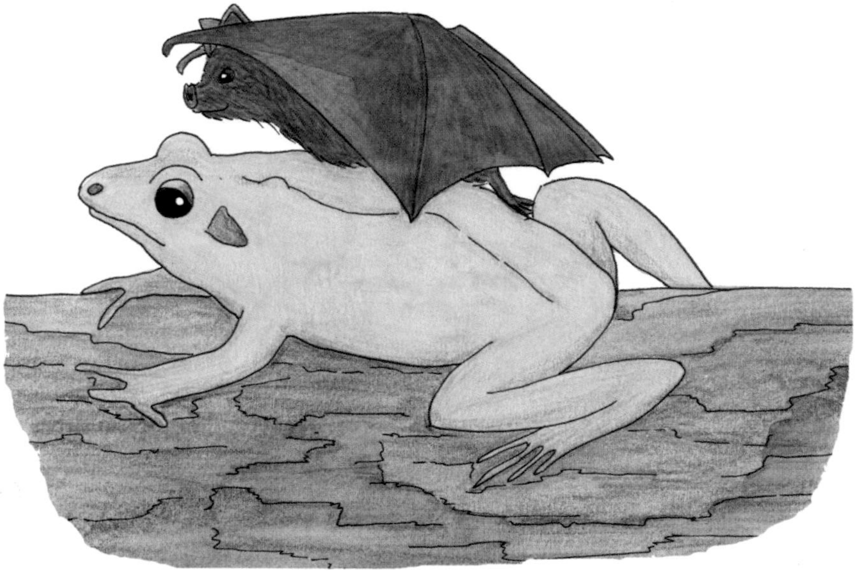

I am on the frog.

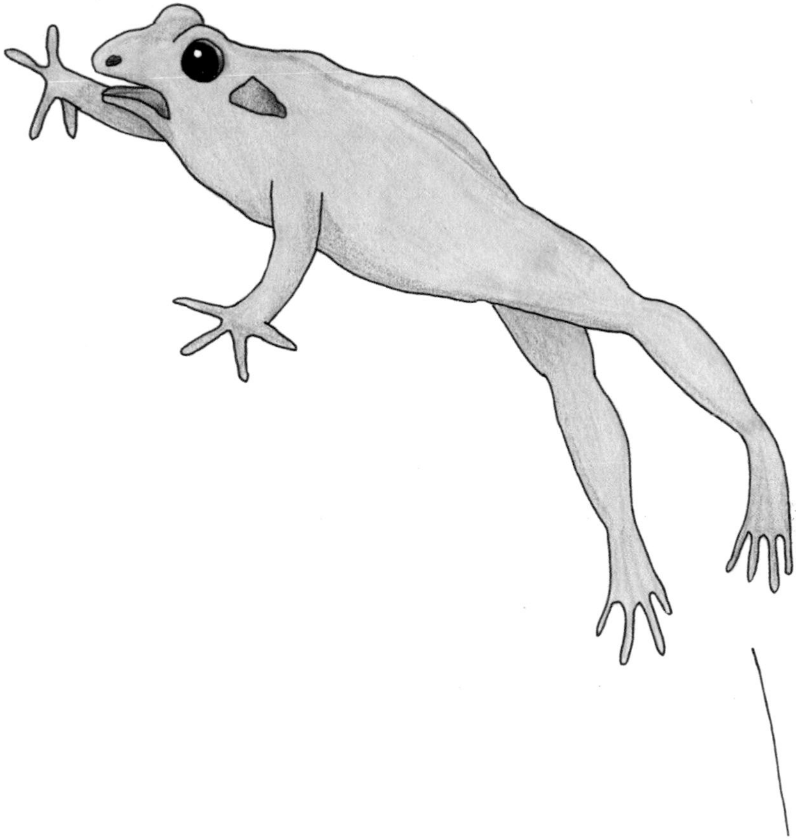

I am mad,
mad, mad.

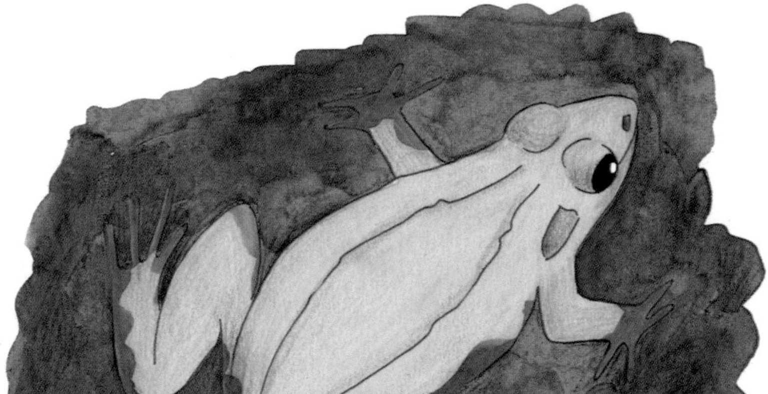

I am in the mud.

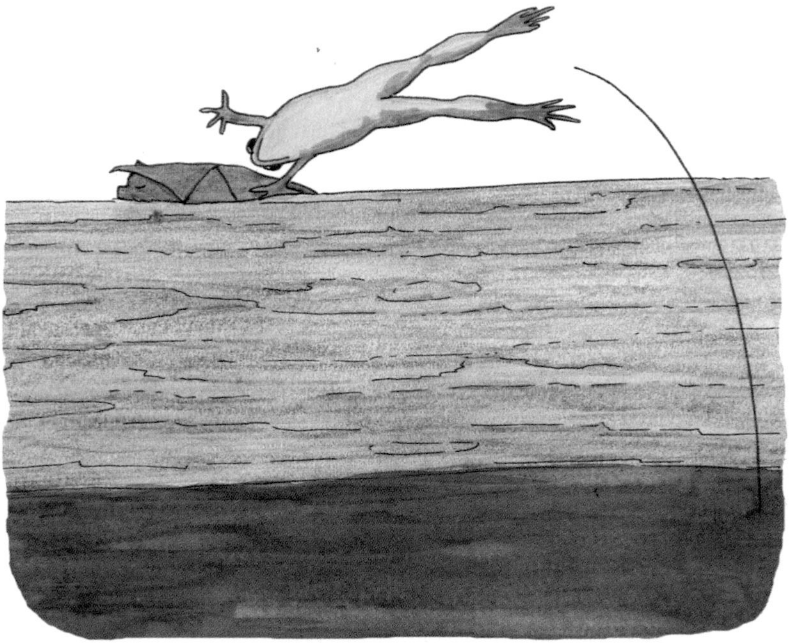

I can hop on
the bat.

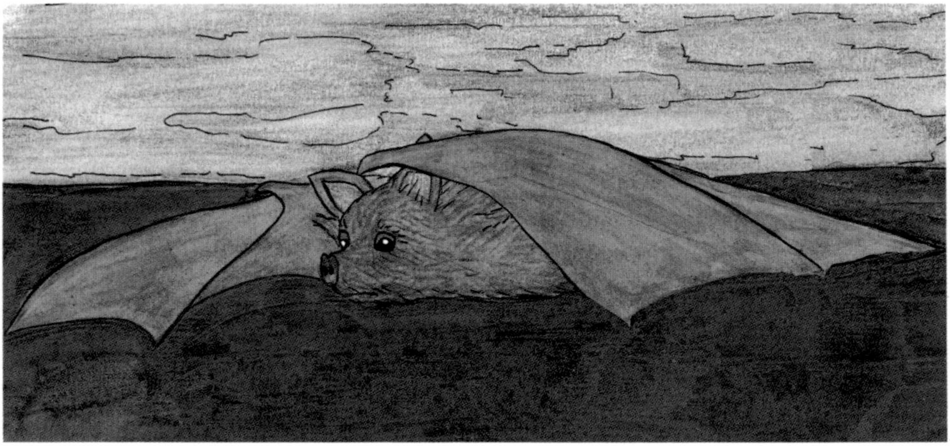

I am sad in the mud.